Tammy Tablespoon

Dana Dipitinsoup

Gary Goldencrust

Franklyn Frenchtoast

Benji Butterslab

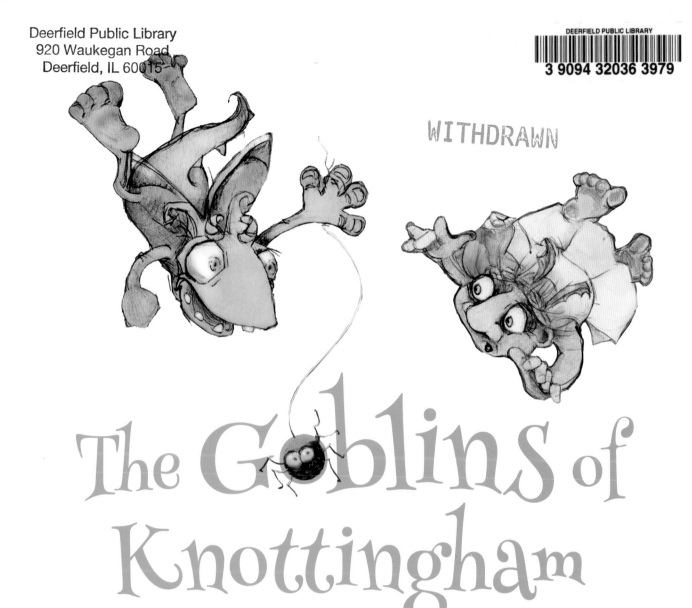

The Goblins of Knottingham

A History of Challah

By Zoë Klein

Illustrated by Beth Bogert

APPLES & HONEY PRESS

Springfield, NJ • Jerusalem

To Rocky, Kinneret, and Zimra:
I loaf you so much. I really dough.
You're fluffy.

To Scott:
Like the flour needs the grain,
you know I knead you.
– ZK

For the Goblin King
and my own two goblins,
Issie and Duncan.
– BB

Author's Note

Judaism has a rich history of stories filled with goblins, ghosts, and ghastly things. You can find these stories in the Talmud and folktales, and in many of them, it is a Jewish ritual object—like the mezuzah, the hamsa, or the knotted fringes of the *tzitzit*—that has the power to protect us from mischief-makers like Knotty, Knotsalot and Notnow. *The Goblins of Knottingham* builds on that age-old tradition.

Apples & Honey Press
An imprint of Behrman House and Gefen Publishing House
Behrman House, 11 Edison Place, Springfield, New Jersey 07081
Gefen Publishing House Ltd., 6 Hatzvi Street, Jerusalem 94386, Israel
www.applesandhoneypress.com

Text copyright © 2017 by Zöe Klein
Illustrations copyright © 2017 by Beth Bogert

ISBN 978-1-68115-526-5

Library of Congress Cataloging-in-Publication Data
Names: Klein, Zoë, author | Bogert, Beth, illustrator.
Title: The goblins of Knottingham : a history of challah / by Zoë Klein ;
   illustrated by Beth Bogert.
Description: Springfield, NJ : Apples & Honey Press, [2017] | Summary: Tired
   of goblins tangling their hair, children fight back, leading to the
   invention of the braided bread called challah.
Identifiers: LCCN 2016032059 | ISBN 9781681155265 (hardcover)
Subjects: | CYAC: Challah (Bread)–Fiction. | Bread–Fiction. |
   Goblins–Fiction. | Hair–Fiction. | Judaism–Customs and practices–Fiction.
Classification: LCC PZ7.1.K648 Go 2017 | DDC [E]–dc23
LC record available at https://lccn.loc.gov/2016032059

Design by Elynn Cohen
Edited by Dena Neusner
Art Directed by Ann D. Koffsky
Printed in China

9 8 7 6 5 4 3 2 1

Long ago, in the town of Knottingham, there were three little goblins named Knotty, Knotsalot, and Notnow.

Knotty was naughty, Knotsalot was no good, and Notnow was no good no how, not then and not now!

They were mean and green
with bulging goopy eyes,
and long gooey fingers,
and bumpy bruised toes.
And they stood about as tall
as your knees to your nose.

There was one thing Knotty, Knotsalot, and Notnow loved to do more than anything else in the world: tangle children's hair!

Every morning, when the children entered school, guess who was hiding in the corner?

That's right! Knotty, Knotsalot, and Notnow, biting their horrid nails and wagging their warted tails. As soon as the bell rang, they would dive headfirst into the children's hair—the longer and looser the better! They twisted it, and tangled it, and tied it into knots. They mussed it and fussed it until every child went home with hair like mops.

And then, the goblins would hoot **hysterically**.

But of course the children did not find it funny **at all!**

Every night they squirmed on stools while their parents yanked and tugged at their messy manes, until their combs snagged and their brushes broke. "Ouch!" the children cried miserably. **"OUCH!"**

"Stay still!" begged their parents, loosening the knots with drippy concoctions of vegetable oil and egg yolk.

"YUCK!"

the children cried miserably.
"YUCK!"

It took so long that there was
no time for homework.
  There was no time for dinner.
  There was no time for PLAY!

One Thursday at recess the children gathered.
"Enough!" the children declared defiantly. "ENOUGH!"

"I hate wearing a hat every day!" hollered Haley Honeydrizzle. "My head gets too hot!"

Tammy Tablespoon told them, "My ponytail is too tight."

And Sara Sesame was silent.

Franklyn Frenchtoast frowned. He
was furious. "We have to fight back!"

But how could the
fed-up friends stop such
sticky, tricky, prickly goblins?

The children thought, and thought, and thought some
more. They scratched their snarled scalps and tried to come
up with a plan. Melissa Mixinchips moved to put mousetraps
in their manes, but Ryan Raisin thought that was really risky.

Sara Sesame stayed silent.

Gary Goldencrust
thought bubble gum
would get them good,
but getting gum out
of hair? Horrible!

Then Dana Dipitinsoup declared, "What about dough?!"

Together, the children devised a daring plan. And it was decided.

The next day was Friday, and all the children wore hats, except for Ryan Raisin.

Patty Punchitdown pulled a big, flat piece of dough from a paper bag.

Haley Honeydrizzle hung it over Ryan Raisin's head. (Ryan was too nervous to refuse.) .

Franklyn Frenchtoast ran a fork firmly over the dough to make fine lines—just like hair. Then the school bell rang, and they went to class.

In the shadows in the corner of the classroom, Knotty, Knotsalot, and Notnow were waiting, biting their horrid nails and wagging their warted tails.

Their eyes roamed the room, looking for a victim.
But all the children were wearing hats.
"This will be no fun, no how!" they thought.

But then, Knotty saw one
child with long, luscious locks.
It was Ryan!

"Follow me!" he howled, and
he dove, fast as a firecracker.

Ryan was really brave! He didn't move an inch.

As Knotty came closer, the goblin sensed something was seriously strange.

He tried to stop, but it was too late!

He zoomed straight into the thick, squishy dough.

"Turn back! It's a trap!" Knotty squealed.

But Knotsalot and Notnow were so close behind they flew right in after him.

Then the children braided the dough tightly around the goblins so they could not escape.

"We got them!" the children cheered. "HOORAY!"

Now what? the children wondered.

"We could bake it," Benji Butterslab said. But braided goblin bread sounded abominable.

"No, no, no!" shouted the goblins.

"We could keep them tied up tight," Tammy Tablespoon stated. "All day and every night."

"Please, no!" groaned the goblins.

Franklyn Frenchtoast suddenly felt sorry for them.

Then Sara Sesame spoke up. "Do you swear to never again tangle children's hair?"

"We swear!" the goblins sobbed.

"Goblins' honor?" Sara asked.

"Goblins' honor!" promised Knotty, Knotsalot, and Notnow.

That day, the good children of
Knottingham let the goblins go, and
Knotty, Knotsalot, and Notnow flew
as far away as their little goblin wings
could carry them.

That night, no one's hair was tugged and yanked
with combs. No one squirmed on stools. Instead, all
the children were tangle-free, and their families finally
had time to laugh and sing over a nice, long meal.

Every Friday since then, the people of Knottingham have made braided, sweet bread called challah to celebrate the end of another tangle free week of school.

The tradition spread from town to town, but the original facts of the story changed over time.

People began to say, "We eat this braided bread because we hope for a tangle-free world, where hands aren't knotted into fists, and eyebrows aren't knotted in confusion, and muscles aren't knotted in stress and pain."

As for Knotty, Knotsalot, and Notnow, they had sworn, on goblins' honor, not to mess up children's hair. But since a goblin's honor is no good no how, not then and not now, they sometimes can't resist a little tangle and twist....
Just not near Knottingham.

The world definitely feels a little happier when you have a hunk of challah in your hand. What do you think gives challah that power?

Is it the smell? After a week of working and thinking hard, we want to unwind. The sweet smell of challah lets us know Shabbat is coming. The little things that bother us (like the goblins in this story!) disappear, and the knots in our muscles and tummies melt away. Yep, that's one powerful smell!

Is it the shape? If you had a sticky, yummy blob of dough in your hands right now, what shape would you make? Challah dough can be made into lots of different shapes. It can be a circle, a ladder, a bird, or anything! When I see a golden loaf of woven strands, the braids remind me of people holding hands and hugging, and that is powerful, too.

Is it the taste? The taste of challah fills the mouth with sweetness, the mind with memories, and the heart with happiness. Some people really like the taste of raisins in their challah. Some prefer chocolate chips. Others prefer plain. What do you like your challah to taste like? Sesame or poppy? Do you like challah drizzled with honey or do you like to use it for French toast?

So, what gives challah its power? Maybe its smell. Maybe its shape or taste. Or maybe its power comes from the people who gather around it, smiling, singing, and sharing stories and filling the world with love.

What chance does a trio of goofy goblins have against *that*?

Toastily,

Rabbi Zoe

PS By the way, did you notice anything funny about the children's names in our story?

Patty Punchitdown

Haley Honeydrizzle

Sara Sesame

Melissa Mixinchips

Ryan Raisin